COMMUNITY · CONNECTIONS

?

WHAT'S IT LIKE TO LIVE HERE?
FISHING VILLAGE
BY KATIE MARSICO

CHERRY LAKE Publishing

Published in the United States of America by Cherry Lake Publishing
Ann Arbor, Michigan
www.cherrylakepublishing.com

Content Adviser: James Wolfinger, PhD, Associate Professor of History,
DePaul University, Chicago, Illinois
Reading Adviser: Marla Conn, ReadAbility, Inc.

Photo Credits: Cover and page 1, ©Hailin Chen/Shutterstock, Inc.; page 5, ©Optikalefx/
Shutterstock, Inc.; page 7, ©photomatz/Shutterstock, Inc.; page 9, ©gary yim/Shutterstock, Inc.;
page 11, ©V. J. Matthew/Shutterstock, Inc.; page 13, ©Rolf_52/Shutterstock, Inc.; page 15,
©Surkov Vladimir/Shutterstock, Inc.; page 17, ©ChameleonsEye/Shutterstock, Inc.; page 19,
©Brigida Soriano/Shutterstock, Inc.; page 21, ©atikinka/Shutterstock, Inc.

LIBRARY OF CONGRESS CATALOGING-IN-PUBLICATION DATA
Marsico, Katie, 1980– What's It Like to Live Here?:
  Fishing village / by Katie Marsico.
    pages cm. — (Community connections)
  Includes bibliographical references and index.
  ISBN 978-1-62431-565-7 (lib. bdg.) — ISBN 978-1-62431-589-3 (ebook) —
ISBN 978-1-62431-581-7 (pbk.) — ISBN 978-1-62431-573-2 (pdf)
  1. Fishing villages—Juvenile literature. I. Title.
  GT5904.M37 2014
  307.76—dc23   2013028552

Cherry Lake Publishing would like to acknowledge the
work of The Partnership for 21st Century Skills. Please
visit www.p21.org for more information.

Printed in the United States of America
Corporate Graphics Inc.
January 2014

FISHING VILLAGE

CONTENTS

WHAT'S IT LIKE TO LIVE HERE?

A WALK ALONG THE WATER

Cindy and her dad grabbed their coats. Outside, the morning was cool and breezy. Seagulls called. Waves crashed nearby. Cindy smelled the ocean. Closer to the water, she smelled fresh fish. Cindy spotted her friend Brandon. He and his mom were feeding water birds. Cindy waved. She loved growing up in a fishing village!

Fishing villages are home to many different water birds, from seagulls to ducks.

Do you know anyone who lives in a fishing village? Maybe you will visit a fishing village someday. If you do, talk with the **residents**. What sights, sounds, smells, and tastes shape their **community**?

5

A fishing village is built along a body of water. People use the water there for **commercial** fishing. Fishing villages are also often home to factories. Fish and seafood are prepared there for sale. Sometimes a village's **economy** is based on **tourism**, too.

Commercial fishers catch large amounts of fish or seafood.

What types of pets do kids in fishing villages own? The most common pets are dogs and cats. Some fishers take their dogs with them to work. The dogs climb aboard the boats to go fishing, too!

Cindy and her dad walked along the dock. The water there was filled with fishing boats. Many fishers were preparing their boats for the day's work. Others were already on their way into the ocean. Cindy knew many of the fishers. The village was very small. Most of its few hundred **residents** knew each other.

The buildings in Lunenburg, Nova Scotia, and other fishing villages are built close to the water.

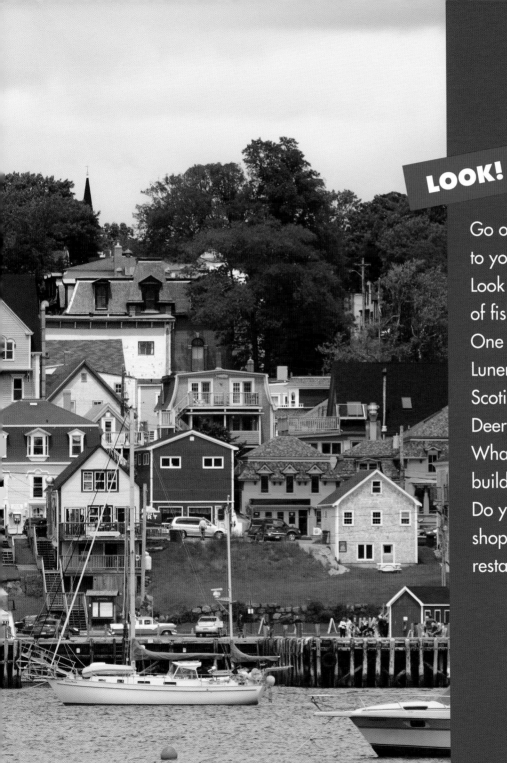

LOOK!

Go online or head
to your local library.
Look up pictures
of fishing villages.
One example is
Lunenburg, Nova
Scotia. Another is
Deer Isle, Maine.
What types of
buildings do you see?
Do you notice any
shops, museums, and
restaurants?

9

SPECIAL TRIP

Cindy and her dad soon reached where the **ferries** docked. They were going to take a ferry to another fishing village nearby. Cindy's dad bought two tickets. They stood in line with other people waiting to board. Cars formed another line. The cars parked on the ferry's bottom deck. People rode in a separate area.

Ferries can carry people between towns along the shoreline.

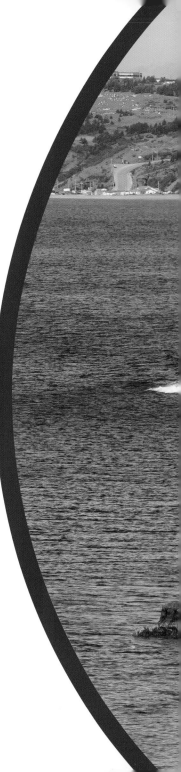

LOOK!

Find photos of ferries on the Internet or in books or magazines. What do these boats carry from shore to shore? They carry a lot more than people! Look carefully. You may find everything from cargo to parked cars.

The trip to the other village was short. Cindy, her dad, and other foot passengers left the ferry first. Then the cars drove off. This fishing village was bigger than Cindy's hometown. It had art galleries and craft shops. There was even a museum about the area's history. That was where Cindy and her dad headed.

Tourists enjoy the shops, museums, and restaurants in fishing villages.

Gather crayons, markers, construction paper, scissors, glue, and poster board. Draw and cut out boats from construction paper. Also draw and cut out buildings found in fishing villages. Paste your boats and buildings on your poster board. This is your very own fishing village model!

13

Cindy was doing a school project about her town. She hoped the museum had information she could use. One part of the museum was about **pollution** in the area. That gave Cindy an idea. Her project could be about cleaning litter from her village's coast! She decided to go straight home to get started.

Keeping the shoreline clear of litter is important for local people and local wildlife.

THINK!

Think about fun experiences that kids have in other communities. What could you do for fun in a farming town? What about in a big city? Can you do these activities in a fishing village?

15

HOME AGAIN

Cindy and her dad walked off the ferry toward home. They stopped to watch fishers bring in their catch. Fishers unloaded crates of haddock and herring. Lobsters and crabs came in on other boats. Cindy's dad explained that fishers in other areas caught other animals. Some fishers brought in salmon and tuna. Others caught shrimp.

Fish are often kept in crates filled with ice until they are sold at market.

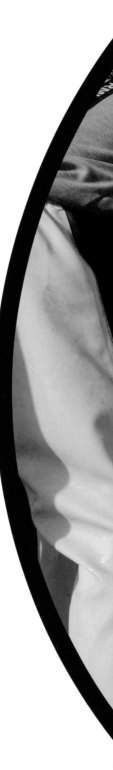

All residents of a fishing village work together. They share fishing waters, harbors, shoreline, and other spaces. They also support their community's economy. This might mean catching seafood. It can also mean attracting visitors. Can you guess other ways neighbors work together?

17

Cindy and her dad finally reached their house. There were still things to do. Cindy's dad was a fisher. He was going fishing the next day. Cindy helped her dad prepare his boat. She made sure the fishing nets were clean and stored.

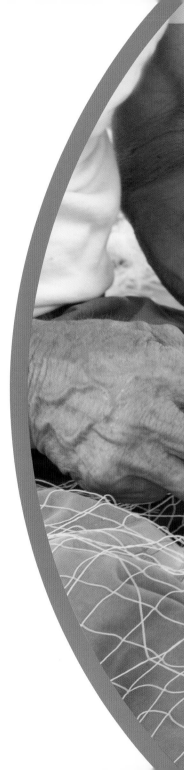

Sometimes a fishing net needs to be mended.

THINK!

What if your parent worked on a fishing boat? Many fishers work from sunrise to sunset. Some go on fishing trips that last several weeks! Fishers travel far across the ocean on these long trips. They face choppy seas and difficult weather.

19

Cindy's dad started making dinner. Cindy took their dog Digby for a walk. Digby would go with Cindy's dad on his trip. Dinner was ready when she got back. It was fresh baked fish and buttered carrots. Her favorite!

A fishing village is a great place to have a dog that loves the water, such as a golden retriever.

ASK QUESTIONS!

Talk to a few people
who have lived in a
fishing village. What
chores are part of
day-to-day life in
their community?
How do their answers
compare to chores
you do?

21

GLOSSARY

cargo (KAHR-go) goods that are carried by a ship or plane

commercial (kuh-MUR-shuhl) having to do with buying and selling things

community (kuh-MYOO-nut-ee) a place and the people who live in it

economy (i-KAH-nuh-mee) a system of buying, selling, making things, and managing money

ferries (FER-eez) boats that regularly carry people, cars, or goods across a body of water

pollution (puh-LOO-shuhn) harmful materials that damage or dirty the air, water, and soil

residents (REZ-uh-dents) people who live in a particular place on a long-term basis

tourism (TOOR-iz-uhm) the business of providing services to visitors and travelers

FIND OUT MORE

BOOKS

Boudreau, Hélène. *Life in a Fishing Community*. New York: Crabtree Publishing, 2010.

Sylvester, Oscar. *Life on a Commercial Fishing Boat*. New York: Gareth Stevens, 2013.

Tieck, Sarah. *Commercial Fishermen*. Edina, MN: ABDO Publishing, 2012.

WEB SITES

Peggy's Cove—A Picturesque Fishing Village in Nova Scotia
www.youtube.com/watch?v=DFLjaMUptAU
Learn all about a fishing village located in Nova Scotia in this video.

Smarter Travel—Ten Fantastic Fishing Villages
www.smartertravel.com/photo-galleries/editorial/10-fantastic-fishing-villages.html?id=183
Check out the profiles of ten popular fishing villages in the United States and Canada.

INDEX

ABOUT THE AUTHOR

Katie Marsico is the author of more than 100 children's books. She lives in a suburb of Chicago, Illinois, with her husband and children.